Books by Robert Coles for young readers

RIDING
FREE

RIDING
FREE

by

ROBERT COLES

3859

An Atlantic Monthly Press Book
Little, Brown and Company   BOSTON   TORONTO

FIRST EDITION

T 09/73

Library of Congress Cataloging in Publication Data

Coles, Robert.
    Riding free.

    SUMMARY: The experiences of two fourteen-year-old
girls who hitchhike to Chicago.
    "An Atlantic Monthly Press book."
    [1. Runaways--Fiction] I. Title.
PZ7.C6777Ri   [Fic]   73-5740
ISBN 0-316-15157-2

ATLANTIC-LITTLE, BROWN BOOKS
ARE PUBLISHED BY
LITTLE, BROWN AND COMPANY
IN ASSOCIATION WITH
THE ATLANTIC MONTHLY PRESS

Published simultaneously in Canada
by Little, Brown & Company (Canada) Limited

PRINTED IN THE UNITED STATES OF AMERICA

To my brother, Bill

RIDING FREE

ON'T ASK ME why I started hitching. Don't ask me to explain what was going on in my head when I walked to a highway a mile from our home and threw out my arm and stuck my thumb up in the air. I remember thinking for a second that my arm and my thumb weren't part of me, that they were out there, telling somebody I wanted a ride, but the rest of me was still in my room, safe and warm and with a bed to sleep in and a kitchen nearby with all the food I'd ever want. I know what *happened;* I'll never forget what happened. But I can't go any further; I can't tell myself it happened because of this reason or that reason.

I was a year younger then. I wasn't anyone special. I was Sallie, spelled like that because my mother said it was a little different, and my dad told her there were a lot of girls named Sally, and why couldn't I have a name no one else had. And that's the difference between them; my mother always says she doesn't want my brother and me to be different from other people, but my father says the world is no good, a lot of it, so we should try to be ourselves, and no one else.

"You're Sallie," he'd tell me, "and no matter if there are a million Sallies in America, none of them is you."

My father and I used to be pretty close. I suppose I was close to my mother, too, but she and my brother Ben were always talking up a storm. Dad and I used to go shopping and we'd take walks and I'd help him clean his car. My mother had a rheumatic heart. The doctor says she'll be all right, live to be a hundred if she takes care of herself, but she has to be careful. That's why my dad and I did the shopping for her. She doesn't like picking things off shelves and carrying packages. She doesn't like cleaning the house very much, either, and when she's upset she clutches at her chest, telling us she can't catch her breath. If she's really upset, she says she's "going," she knows it, she's *"going."*

4

"Stop, just *stop*." I remember my father saying that. I wasn't sure whether he was talking to my mother or to me. Was he ordering me to stay or was he ordering my mother to shut up and quit threatening us with her rheumatic heart?

That day! That day started like any other day. I got up, I started getting dressed. I looked at my face in the mirror and wished I were as pretty as Rita next door. She has a name I don't like, but I'd gladly be a Rita if I could look like her. I washed, got dressed, and went downstairs. Then it began. My father didn't like my dress. "It's not right for school. You look like you're going to a masquerade!" He didn't just say it, he shouted it; and my mother's hand went to her chest. "When did you get *that*? *Where*? I'm not going to pay the bill! Take it back — today, right after school."

I thought I was dreaming. Mother told me I could buy a couple of dresses, and she said any dress they carried in the dress shop, in our town's shop, was all right with her.

I think she originally *liked* what I bought. But she's scared of him, scared as can be of Daddy — that's what I thought when I saw her head bob up and down, two or three times, like a nice, obliging little girl. Oh, Mother, I wanted to say; stand up for yourself, for me, and don't back down, panting and holding on to yourself and telling us you're sick and going to die.

"I like it," I screamed, "so mind your own business!"

"It *is* my business!" he shouted back, and he slammed that morning paper of his down on the table. I stared right back at him. I looked into his eyes, and for a second I thought he was going to smile at me and drop the subject. But no, he raised his voice and started on a sermon: everything is turning bad these days, and I'd better watch out, or I'll ruin myself before I know it.

Oh, he went on and on, but I can't remember the words. All I can see now is his face, red and a sweat breaking out, and his hand wiping his forehead with a napkin. When he gets nervous he wipes his forehead.

I can still hear my own words: "I'm wearing this; it's on, and it'll stay on."

The next thing I knew he was pulling me back to my bedroom. "No, no."

"Yes," he kept on saying.

I was moving toward the bedroom, maybe giving in; I don't know. But suddenly my mother dropped a plate and started crying, and we both forgot our argument and went to her. My brother came running downstairs, too. Up to then he must have been sitting in that room of his smiling and enjoying the fight.

In a second or two we were all beside Mother. She was pale, and she was having trouble breathing. Dad sat her down and held her hand and told Ben and me to leave the room. In a few minutes he called us back. She was better, and I thought I'd be able to go to school in peace. But no, Dad was determined to keep after me. "Go and put on something re-spectable!"

"*This* is respectable; it's what all the girls are wearing."

"Do as I say."

I didn't know, even then, how serious he was. My father can say things, then seem to forget his own words. But he *was* serious. "I won't leave this house until you change into something else." I still thought he was half-pretending; I didn't think he would really miss his train. But he didn't leave and he didn't leave, and I got scared.

I still wasn't going to change my clothes. Dad said he'd stay home all day, if need be — because I wasn't going out of the house looking like that. It got later and later. He missed his train and I knew I was going to be late for school. I started crying, and Dad kept wiping his forehead and talking. "What's come over you, Sallie? You used to be a good girl. We had such good times together. Now you dress like a tramp, you're on the phone half the night. You sit in that room talking with those girl friends of yours about the stupidest things, and I can't believe I'm hearing my daughter, my own daughter. You're fourteen now. Soon you'll be fifteen. For God's sake wake up and get down to business. Your grades have been going down, down, down. You mope around and give that mirror of yours so much business I'm surprised it still works. Who pays for all these clothes? Why don't you go get a job after school, and buy your own clothes? Then you can wear what you want.

But as long as I'm paying the bills, *as long as I'm paying the bills . . ."*

Oh, he went on and on, repeating himself over and over, until I was sick and shaking and trying not to cry. We'd had worse fights, one about the telephone. My father burst into my room and said he would rip the wire out of the wall if I didn't hang up. I did; I hung up and ran out of the house and went over to Sue's. I spent the night there, too. I called and my mother was crying and my father grabbed the phone and told me I could stay with Sue for a month — a year; he didn't care. I came home the next day and all was forgotten, except that it wasn't.

This time I couldn't go to Sue's, though. She was in school. So I changed into jeans, and when my father saw me come out of my room he made a face but offered to drive me to school so I wouldn't be late. I said no. I walked out of the house and didn't say goodbye to him — or to my mother either.

"Nonsense," my father always says, and he's been right, so far. The last thing I heard when I was leaving the house was my mother crying — and telling me she was going to die. "If you leave, I won't call the police. I don't want to keep you here by force. I'll pray that you'll come right back. I only hope to stay alive. I can go any minute. I know one day I'll just go, and that will be that."

'D BEEN hitching before. Sue and I would leave school and wait by the road and some of the boys would pick us up. It was more fun doing it that way than arranging with them for a ride home. We'd turn them down in school, then let them pick us up on the road, a block or two away.

I'd never hitched alone, and I'd never even dreamed of hitching near my home. That morning I waited for the bus and waited and it didn't come. I walked to the highway and I held out my hand. I wasn't in the least afraid. The next thing I knew I had a ride. A man pulled over in a big green car, a Cadillac. He asked me where I was going, and I said school.

"Where is that?"

All of a sudden I heard myself saying Jordan Valley Junior College.

"I'm going by there. I'll drop you off."

"Thank you."

For a minute or so, he didn't say anything, and I wasn't going to say anything, either. As we passed the turnoff for school, all of a sudden I felt awkward and almost scared. He took a right at the fork. In half an hour I'd be there, at the college.

"You smoke?" he asked me.

"No, sir."

"No one calls me 'sir.' But it's nice to see some respect from young people. I can't get over what is happening these days — the way college kids behave. I'm only thirty-six, but I feel like I'm eighty when I see these hippie types near our colleges. I guess you're not a hippie, are you?"

"No, sir, I don't believe I am."

"Well, you're hitchhiking, aren't you? I wouldn't want my daughter to do that. You know what kind of women hitchhike? You know what a man like me, driving along, is bound to think, when he sees a pretty, young girl like you standing there, all alone, asking for a ride?"

Listening to him, I began to shake. I stared out

the window and pretended I didn't even hear him. Then I began to smell smoke, and I thought maybe the car was on fire. I turned from looking out the window and counting the stores we passed, and looked over at him. There he was, chewing on a cigar. It suddenly occurred to me that I hadn't even seen him until now. He had blond hair and a blue suit on. I figured he must be a businessman, what with the big car and the cigar and the way he was talking. Maybe he's a racketeer, I thought. I turned toward the window again. I held on to the armrest. Then I felt the lever that opens the door and I decided to hold it with my right hand. If anything happened, I could open the door. Then maybe a policeman would see what was happening, and stop the car.

I was thinking like a two-year-old. The man didn't say another word for the whole ride. He pulled up in front of the college and let me out. I thanked him, and he nodded and pulled away real fast. I was still scared, but I was proud of myself.

Now I could walk around the college and no one

would bother me. No one knew where I was — and I was glad. I passed a few girls and tried to look casual, as if I were a student there, but I kept thinking of my father and my mother and all the trouble at home. And the more I thought, the angrier I got. I tried to picture myself going home and apologizing, the way my father would expect me to and my mother would plead with me to do — but I couldn't, I wouldn't do it. Not this time. This was the millionth time my father had shouted at me and told me I was doing the wrong thing and was headed for no good. That's his expression: "You're headed for no good."

As I was walking past a big building, the gym maybe, a tall woman with gray hair came toward me. She was carrying an umbrella so I looked up at the sky and saw how cloudy it was. Then I worried that she might spot me as a stranger. I didn't have any books and the college wasn't very big, so the teachers must know most of the kids. I wanted to look at her and smile, but I quickly looked away. She said hello, and I mumbled back.

I knew my girl friend Sue had a cousin at the college, Nancy. I had forgotten her last name. Sue always called her Nan. If I could find her, I could stay in her room until Sue got out of school and came home. Then I could call her. I walked and walked and looked and looked at the girls, but no luck. I was getting hungry and I wondered where I could get something to eat. I didn't know where the cafeteria was. It was getting toward noon, and I was tired and I began to wish I was back in school. In school! I said to myself: Sallie, count your blessings. At least you've missed one day of those dumb teachers, going over and over the same old stuff and sounding as bad as your mother and father. I will never be like them, *never!* I must have sworn that to myself a thousand times that day.

Finally it was three o'clock. I saw a phone booth and went into it and called Sue, and thank God she was home.

"Sue."

"Sallie!"

"Sue." I repeated her name because I felt as though she was far away and I was making a long-distance call. And I was so glad to hear her voice that I just wanted to say her name again.

"Sallie, where are you? Where were you today? Are you sick? What's the matter?"

"No, I'm O.K. There's nothing wrong."

"Why didn't you come to school today?"

"It's a long story. Where are you, Sue?"

"Where *am* I? Sallie, what's the matter with you? I'm home. You just called me."

"I mean, can we get together and talk — right now? The phone is no good. I want to see you."

"Sallie, what is wrong? Where are you? I'll be right over."

"Sue, I'm not home. I'm here — I'm at Jordan Valley, at the college."

"Sallie! What are you doing there?"

"I want to see *you*, Sue. Can't you come over here now?"

"Sallie! It's not next door; you're a half-hour drive away, maybe an hour, something like that. I can't just walk over there."

"You can get a ride."

"Sallie! Are you *really* there? You're kidding me.

You're really at home! You're in bed, I know it. You sound as if you've got the flu. I'll be right over."

"No, no, Sue; I'm not at home. I'm right here. I'm at Jordan Valley, I swear. Don't go near my house, you hear! Come over here. You can hitch a ride, like I did."

"When did you do that?"

"This morning."

"You've been there all day?"

"Yes, it's been a few hours."

"Sallie, it's supposed to rain any minute. Why don't you come back — come over here, and we can talk!"

"No. I'm not going back. If I come to see you, it'll mean I'll have to go home. You wait and see, my mother will be calling your house soon, any minute. You come here, Sue. I've got to talk with you."

"I can't hitch alone. I've never done that. I'll try and get my brother to drive me over. Just wait there. I'll try to get over as soon as I can."

"Sue, don't hang up! I'll be near the front gate. I'll meet you there. O.K.?"

"O.K."

SHE CAME. It took her over an hour, but she came. Her brother dropped her off, and I could see them trying to figure out how the two of us would get back. I ran over to the car. I was never so glad in my life to see anyone. I hugged her. I said hello to her brother, and he said if I wanted to come back now, he could drive us. I said no; we could both hitch back. Sue wanted us to go right back with her brother, I could tell, but she saw that I wouldn't agree, so she told him to go home and we'd come back soon.

Then we walked and walked and talked and talked. Sue kept on telling me I was wrong. "I agree with you, but there's nothing we can do with our parents except tolerate them. They're just out of it, and they don't *understand*. But you can't run away. That's not the answer. That's wrong. Where can you go? What can you do?"

"I can leave. I'm going to be fifteen in a few months. I don't have to sit back and be insulted. I can go out and get a job. I can do something."

"Sallie, you're losing your mind. You're talking silly. They could track you down; they could call the police. It's only a few more years, then we can get away. We can come here, to Jordan Valley, like Nan did. She didn't like *her* father for a long time, I remember. Or her mother, either!"

"Listen, Sue, this place is too close to home. My mother would be calling me up all the time, telling me she's worried over me, and she's not feeling too good, and all that. And my father would want to check up on me. What are you wearing? Who are you going out with? Who are your friends? Are you studying? I'm not sending you there for a vacation! Oh, I can hear him. I don't want to listen to that stuff again, ever again."

"Sallie, come on home to my house. We can spend the night there. I'll call and ask my mother."

I said no, and I kept on saying no. Sue started to give in. Finally: "Where could we go, supposing we wanted to leave home. Where would we *stay?*"

"I have a cousin in Chicago; we could stay with her. It's better than staying with *your* cousin, right here, practically in our own backyard. My cousin is twenty-four. She has a job. She could put us up, I'm sure. She used to baby-sit with me. I liked her. She was always good to Ben and me. She even writes us letters sometimes. She could give us a place to stay and we could look for a job, something like that. Or we could phone home and say we'll be back, but they've got to stop treating us like babies. They've got to realize we're grown up, and that's that!"

Sue agreed with me, but she still wanted to know what we could do in Chicago. I kept on telling her we could just visit and look around. "One thing at a time, Sue," I must have said twenty-five times.

The funny thing was that Sue admitted it to me — her parents were even worse than mine, if that's possible. "You have it easy, Sallie. You haven't heard your father shouting and throwing things — anything he can lay his hands on. The man is crazy sometimes."

"That's why we've got to go away. It'll teach them a lesson. Look, Sue, we don't have to stay for the rest of our lives. We have a week's vacation coming up next week, anyway, so we wouldn't be missing much school. And what would we do at home during that vacation? You know. You'd be in tears every day, and so would I. Remember the time *you* said we should run away? Then it was *me* who said we should wait. But I'm tired of waiting. I think we ought to stand up and show them that we're not going to take it anymore."

"Right, right. But when do we go? How do we get to Chicago? I haven't got enough money to get home from here, never mind Chicago. That's five hundred miles away."

"I have ten dollars and some change, too. All we need to do is stick out our thumbs, and the next thing you know we'll be in Chicago. I could call my cousin now. Or no — maybe I'd better not. She might get worried and phone my parents. It's best to get there, then call her and tell her we want to come over and talk."

"Sallie, I think we ought to wait until tomorrow. I mean, we need clothes, and we need money. I can borrow some from my brother. All we have now is your ten dollars and the clothes on our backs. We have to go home and plan."

"No. That's foolish. You don't *plan* to run away.

You just *go*. Look, all we need is a couple of rides. Who knows, we might get one ride, and the driver could be going right to Chicago. We don't need clothes just to go visit my cousin. Let's just go. We can have fun! You're trying to make this into a big trip, an expedition to Europe or something."

Sue started crying. Her parents would go crazy when she didn't show up for supper and she was sure the police would come and get us, wherever we were, and then we'd be in real trouble. But she decided to stay with me, and I was glad. I never would have had the courage to hitchhike to Chicago alone — not then, knowing as little as I did about the road. I would have been too scared. It's one thing to hitchhike alone from your house to Jordan Valley Junior College. It's another thing to go on the Interstate and try to get to a big city like Chicago — all by yourself.

Together we felt safe. The first ride was easy — almost as if we were back at high school. Lots of boys come to Jordan Valley and one stopped and asked us where we were going. To the Interstate, I said. Sue grabbed my hand and clutched it. I was a little nervous myself but I knew I had to hide it from Sue. If she had seen any sign that I didn't know *exactly* what we were going to do, she would have started crying, and that would have been the end of our trip to Chicago.

The boy was nice. He wanted to know how far we were going on the Interstate, because if it wasn't too far, he'd take us. "To Chicago," I said.

"Chicago!"

"Yes, Chicago. Have you heard of it?"

"Sallie!"

"You're both going there, all the way to Chicago — hitching?"

"That's right — that's where we're going."

Sue didn't like the way I was talking with him. She tried to be as nice as he was. She asked him where he came from and what he was majoring in and all that stuff. He kept looking over at the two of us, and I could tell he was wondering how old we were and why we weren't going home, instead of all the way to Chicago. And the more Sue talked with him, the worse it was going to be when he left us off — I could see that. Sue would want to stay with him, and get him to take us to her house or mine!

Fortunately the Interstate wasn't far away. He pulled over and said there was no use taking us a little up the road, because we were now at a good spot to catch a ride, so he'd just let us off right there.

"Good," I said, and I started pushing on Sue so she'd open the door. She hesitated, just as I expected, but when I pushed harder she moved her right arm and opened up that door.

"Take care of yourselves," the boy said.

"Take care of *yourself*," I yelled as he drove away.

"You didn't even thank him, Sallie."

"Well, I told him to take care of himself."

"But the way you said it! He was just trying to be a gentleman, that's all."

"O.K. I guess I *was* rude. Here we are, though. Let's try and catch a good ride before it starts to rain and gets dark."

We stood there. It was already dark — dark enough and cold enough to make me wish I was back home in my room, lying on my bed and listening to records.

I almost turned to Sue and said, "Let's go home," but I didn't. Maybe she was reading my mind, or maybe, like me, she suddenly became homesick, because she said to me, "Sallie, let's go home."

I felt the words coming to my lips, "Yes, O.K.," but I fought them back. I could hear my father's long lecture on how bad I was to run away, and how my allowance was going to be cut off, and I couldn't play my records. Mother would be standing there crying and saying, "Please, you two, please don't fight." A lot of good she is when she's really needed! No, I said to myself, I'm going to Chicago if I have to walk all the way.

"No, Sue. But you can go home if you want to. Don't worry about me."

"Well, I *am* worrying about you. You can't hitchhike on a highway like this all by yourself."

"Why can't I?"

"You'll get hurt. There's no telling *who* will pick you up, and what he'll try to do."

"Stop being a nut. I can take care of myself. If worse comes to worst I'll jump in the back while he's driving, and if he slows down, I'll leap out before he stops and signal other cars for help. Besides, you only get into trouble if you're looking for it."

"Sallie, I can't figure you out. You *know* there are crazy people driving cars. A lot of girl hitchhikers have been beaten and raped. There was one in the paper the other day. Let's go home and figure out how we can go visit your cousin; we could borrow money and take the bus. Maybe she'd send us some money. We could go during the vacation. My father *might* give us the money as a present. He's always telling me I should see how other people live in different parts of the country, and then I wouldn't complain so much."

"Stop. Stop it, Sue. You should go home, right now. I'd offer to hitch back with you, so you wouldn't be in any danger, but I've got to get to Chicago, and I have no time to spare. Besides, my father may have the police out looking for me. When I get to Chicago my cousin will call my parents and then they'll know where I am. But don't worry about me, Sue. You go home, and I'll call you when I get to Chicago."

"No, I'm staying with you."

"Sue, you don't have to."

"I know I don't have to. I want to."

"O.K. O.K."

CARS HAD BEEN tearing past all the while we were talking, but I hadn't really paid attention to them. Now I looked at each one. It was dusk, and some had their lights on and some didn't. We just stood there, not saying a word to each other. The cars were disappearing into the coming night. They were becoming headlights rushing toward us and then in a flash disappearing, replaced by red taillights. Each car brought a slam of wind, and each truck an engine's roar and even a slight trembling of the pavement where we stood. I tried to play games with myself. I tried to predict which car would stop. *This* one, I'd say, and the big Oldsmobile or Buick would go by fast. That one won't stop, and it didn't, the Volkswagen. Then a truck appeared and I got worried. What should we do if the driver stops? We'd be way up there, and there's no back seat, just that place where the man sits behind the huge steering

26

wheel. I'd never been in a truck before and I was afraid of truck drivers. Maybe I'd seen too many television shows or movies; the truck drivers in them seem tough.

The truck went by, though; and so did more trucks and a lot of cars, too. Sue and I began to worry. I didn't say anything to her, and she didn't say anything to me, but we each knew what the other was thinking: would we have to stand there all night, and get colder and colder and get nowhere? But then a car came toward us and slowed, and we were sure we had our ride, at last. The man looked at us, *stared* at us. He stopped. We ran toward the car. We were almost at the door — it was a Ford — when all of a sudden he gunned the car and was off at about sixty or eighty before Sue or I could figure out what happened.

"What happened, Sallie?"

"I don't know."

"I'm glad he didn't give us a ride if he's like that!"

"Like what, Sue?"

"I don't know — crazy. Why should a man stop

and then take off like that? Do you think he's a cop, in an unmarked car? Do you think he's going to get the police?"

"Don't be foolish. He was sizing us up, that's what. I suppose if just one of us were here, he'd have picked me up, or you, and tried to take us someplace, maybe to a motel up the road."

"Sallie! Do you think so? How do you know?"

"I *don't* know; but I can guess. Why else would he pull over and then pull away? He wanted to see us, and then he probably decided he couldn't get very far with the *two* of us."

"Well, I told you it was dangerous to do this, Sallie."

"You can still go back, Sue. Don't worry about me."

Sue didn't say a word. She kicked a stone and then she picked up a bigger stone and threw it on the road.

"Maybe that will make them stop!" She grinned at me, and I tried to smile back, and we didn't say anything. We just held up our right hands and kept our thumbs pointed up and the next thing we knew, a car pulled up. We ran toward it and the man was leaning over, holding open the door. It was a red Volkswagen, fairly new. We didn't hesitate a second; we just piled in, Sue in the back and I sat up front.

"Where are you going?" he said.

"To Chicago," I said.

"All the way to Chicago?"

"Yes."

"I sure can't take you there. But I'm going twenty miles up the road and I can leave you off at a good place for hitching. Of course, it's nearly nighttime, so you may have your troubles. If you're lucky a truck driver will pick you up and take you right into the Loop, and maybe even buy you a few meals on the way."

"Where's the Loop?" Sue asked.

"You're going to Chicago and you don't know where the Loop is!"

"She hasn't been to Chicago. My cousin lives there, and we're visiting her. She's on Dorchester Avenue, I believe. She's listed in the phone book. I've been to Chicago and visited her there, but it was a few years ago. I don't know if we went to the Loop or not."

"The Loop is the downtown shopping area in Chicago. I know Chicago. I lived there four years, went to college there. You girls are going to be plenty cold when you get there. It's still winter there, now. The wind comes in off the lake and it can blow you down. And there's no telling how late they get snow. This rain we're starting to get — it could be snow up in Chicago. Of course, they can get an early spring, too."

It *was* raining. We were lucky to get the ride when we did! I looked over at the driver — it was the first chance I had to more than glance at him. He seemed to be about twenty-five, maybe less. He looked like the college graduate he said he was: a tweed jacket and a raincoat that probably was made in England. He wore those horn-rimmed glasses. I tried to see if he had a wedding ring on his left hand, but it was wrapped around the steering wheel, and I could only give a quick glance, then pretend to look out the window — even though by now the outside was pitch-black, and all you could see were the faraway lights in homes or shopping centers or the taillights on cars up ahead or the twin lights coming toward us. For a few minutes no one said anything. I looked to see if there was a radio in the car, and there was. I figured that any second he'd put it on, and that would make it easier. We could relax and enjoy the ride, and we wouldn't have to think up things to say. But the man wanted to talk. He introduced himself, told us his name was Jim, Jim Hunt, and that he was born in Chicago and grew up in St. Louis, and had been visiting his sister in Pennsylvania, and soon he was going to California, because he was an engineer and he had a job out there. Sue told him her father was an engineer, and they talked about which engineering schools were good, and where the best jobs were. I began to like the guy. He was kind, and he wasn't trying to scare us about hitching. He told us what to see in Chicago, and he said he'd hitched all across the country when he was in college.

"Of course it's different now. In the last few years

more and more young people, like you two, are out on the road. And it's amazing, the number of girls you see — almost as many as boys."

Then he turned to me and asked me how long I'd been hitching.

"I just started."

"You've never hitched before?"

"Oh, I've hitched to school and back, and around the neighborhood, but never on a big highway like this."

"Well, there's nothing to be afraid of, I guess. It's good there are two of you." He paused, and I could see that he wanted to say something more. He glanced at me, then he looked in his mirror. He was driving in the middle lane, and he moved toward the right-hand lane. He looked at his watch. Then he spoke up: "It's too bad you two have to travel by night. It's much easier to catch a ride by day. I suppose if you're lucky someone will stop who is driving right through the night to Chicago. But you may not get any ride, and you'll be standing there hour after hour, and it's raining. I'm supposed to turn off about five miles ahead, but I can't leave you there. In the daytime it's a good spot, but not at night. I'm going to take you about eight or ten miles farther. There's a gas station there, and a restaurant — it's open all night. You can sit and have coffee and ask around for a lift. I used to do that on Route 66. I remember I was in Albuquerque and I was standing and standing and getting nowhere. So I went into a restaurant and I had some coffee, and when I saw some people getting ready to go, I went up to them and told them I needed a ride real bad, and my dad was sick and I was trying to get home to see him. Sure, they said, and the next thing I knew I was in Los Angeles. Now, you don't strike oil like that every time, but sometimes you do, especially if you're not shy, and you keep your eyes open. Those people even bought me meals. I tried to pay for my own. I even tried to buy *them* a meal or two, but no, they wouldn't hear of it."

He went on and on, telling us about his experiences until we pulled into the station. He was going to get gas and then we would all go for supper. Sue and I looked at each other — and I guess he read our thoughts. "Don't worry. Please don't. I've had a lot of favors done me while hitching across this country. I don't have anything to do right now. I'm on my way to visit my aunt and uncle. They're both quite sick, and to tell you the truth, I dread spending more than an hour or two with them. I'll call them from the restaurant and tell them I'll be late because of the traffic and the weather, and I'll see them before they go to bed. If they weren't sick, I'd ask you girls to come over and spend the night there. Then I could take you to the highway early in the morning and you'd be able to travel to Chicago in daylight."

When he had first started to talk I thought he was a real smoothie, a college-educated smoothie, and I was going to whisper to Sue when we pulled into the gas station that we *had* to get away from him. But the more he talked the more I liked him — and trusted him. Of course Sue was all wrapped up in him, I could tell. Poor Sue, she's a baby. She believes anything she hears. When we were younger I used to tell her I'd gone to Europe over the weekend with my dad, and she believed me. Once my brother told Sue he was going to take both of us up to the moon, and she asked him when, and she wasn't *pretending* to be gullible. That was when she lived next door to us — and we were about five or six, I guess.

The gas station was big, with a restaurant and a motel. It was quite a place, all lighted up, and with lots and lots of cars. I was glad to be there, and I really looked forward to going into the restaurant. Suddenly I felt hungry, real hungry, and I remembered that I hadn't eaten all day. Plenty of times I've tried to starve myself — stay away from food all the way from breakfast until supper. But my sweet tooth always got the better of me. But this time I had missed lunch and I hadn't even thought of food once since then — until now.

"What are you going to order?" Sue asked me before we even sat down at a table.

"A dozen cheeseburgers and a dozen orders of french fries and three or four milk shakes."

"Why don't you girls sit over at that table. I'm going to call my aunt. Order me a club sandwich and coffee."

We sat down, and when the waitress came we each ordered one and only one cheeseburger.

"I thought you were hungry, Sallie."

35

"I *am,* but I don't want to spend the money."

"I have some. I have five dollars. I didn't want to tell you."

"Keep it. We may need it. He'll want to pay for our supper, I know. I hate the way he treats us — calling us 'girls' and giving us little lectures. He must be in training to be a lawyer or a minister."

"How do you know that? I think he's very nice."

"I'm not saying he isn't nice. He's a little *too* nice, if you ask me."

"Sallie, you're being cruel. The guy wants to help us, and you talk about him that way!"

"What have I said against him? I'm glad he picked us up. He's all right. He's fine. I trust him. But just because someone gives you a ride doesn't mean you have to fall in love with him! I'm going to thank him, don't worry!"

"Well, I think he's nice. He's nicer than some of the guys we hang around with. They're children — *babies.* We're getting older, Sallie. My father is seven years older than mother. Nearly eight years. We spend too much time with boys our own age, and they're really about ten — I mean, their minds haven't developed."

"Oh, my God, she's fallen in love, she really has. Poor Sue, a man comes along and gives her a ride and offers to buy her supper, and he has on a tweed jacket and a pipe in the pocket — with tobacco in it, I'm sure, and not pot — and the next thing you know Sue is walking down the aisle of her church, ready to say yes, yes, yes."

"Stop it," she giggled. "What are *you* planning to do? I'd rather dream of marriage than spend my time hitchhiking all over the country."

"Go home! You can go right home, right now! Why don't you tell your friend when he comes back to the table — and I'm sure he'll want to drive you all the way home, to the front door. I didn't ask you to come, Sue. And as far as I'm concerned . . ."

"Please, Sallie. I didn't mean to sound that way. We're tired and hungry and I'm a little scared. You're not, but I am. It's better to be honest . . ."

Then the man came back. He'd called his aunt and he was hungry, too. We had to wait longer than we should have for the food, and it wasn't the best, but it filled us up and Sue and I felt better. For a few seconds I found myself wishing that we could just sit there all night, and maybe go next door and get a room in the motel and sleep a little bit, and then start out fresh in the morning. But I wanted to get to Chicago; I *really* wanted to get there. While Sue and the man were talking about food and the weather and colleges and what kind of automobile is safe to drive, I pictured myself in an airplane. I was a stowaway. The plane landed in Chicago, and then I got out and no one noticed me and my cousin was waiting for me, where people do, at a gate in a big terminal building. When Sue asked me what I was thinking about, I shook my head. I waited for a few seconds, then I asked the man where the nearest airport was.

"No place near here. Why?"

"Yes, why, Sallie?"

"No reason. I just was wondering. Wouldn't it be nice if we could fly to Chicago."

"I know what you mean. It's a tough night for

driving, never mind hitchhiking. I dread the short drive to my aunt's. Speaking of that, I'd better get going."

He paid the bill, said goodbye to us, and left.

SUE AND I sat at the table and stared at each other — neither of us anxious to go out into the wet, dark outside. We saw some other kids who looked about our age sitting at the counter, and we decided to ask them for a ride. Sue said I was better at talking to strangers, and she was right — but to be better at it than Sue wasn't much. I sat there figuring out what I would say and the longer I thought out the words, the worse it got. I finally decided to get up and walk over and say whatever came to my head. I looked at the kids lined up on the counter stools and decided not to pick one out in advance; I could have spent the whole night deciding which one to ask, and why. Instead, I walked over and let my body stop wherever it happened to stop.

It stopped in front of a guy who wasn't like the

man who had brought us to the restaurant. He was what my father would call a hippie — and he was what *I* would call a freak. I mean, he wasn't like some of the boys my father tells me look "far out." He was *way* out! He had a band around his forehead, and his hair wasn't just long, it was flowing. I don't think I meant to talk with him. It was just that as I came near the counter, he turned toward me and asked: "Need help?" I thought he was joking, and for a minute I wanted to ignore him, or tell him to shut up and mind his own business. But he smiled, and that was when I asked him the question —

"Are you by any chance going toward Chicago?"

"We're going to San Francisco and you're welcome to come with us. If you want to leave in Chicago, that's O.K., too." I just stood there. It was too easy and I didn't know what to say next. Then the girl beside him spoke.

"We have a car. You can come with us, but we're not going much farther tonight. We're camping out a little way up the road. There's no use rushing."

She had on a blue work shirt and dungarees. She

had a pretty face, but her hair was wet and stringy, as though she'd been walking in the rain. I decided it was easier to go along with them than turn away and try someone else farther down the counter. Anyway, they all looked alike — the kids sitting there. The grownups looked like businessmen or truck drivers and I didn't have the nerve to approach them.

"I'll go get my friend," I said and just stood there stupidly until I realized that the girl was staring at me. I left and went over to Sue. I told her I had a ride and tried to tell her who the people were without pointing at them. Sue got worried again, for the hundredth time.

"Sallie, not them. I'm against it. I think there are four or five of them traveling together — not just the two you talked to. What kind of a car do they have? How could we fit in? What kind of people are they?"

If I had any doubts, Sue settled them. "Look, Sue, what do you want? Do you expect a Cadillac will pull up here, in front of the restaurant, and a chauffeur will come in and page us? He'd drive us to

Chicago and hand us each a brand-new one-hundred-dollar bill when we step out — right in front of my cousin's apartment house. Or is it a plane you want, the President's jet, maybe?"

"Stop, Sallie. Please, let's not fight. I don't want to be a pain, but those people look as if they've been around, all over the place. They aren't our kind."

She was right, and now that she put it that way I felt myself melting. For a second I felt like crying; it was like a wave that came over me. I had to stop feeling like that.

"Sue, they won't hurt us. We can always part company if we don't like them. There's no law that says we have to stay with people just because they give us a ride. But they seem to know how to travel, and they have a car, and they have a tent, I think. We'd be better off with them than standing somewhere on the Interstate half the night with the rain coming down."

"O.K."

We both went over and they introduced themselves, the girl and the boy and another girl and another boy, and we introduced ourselves, and we followed them over to their car, an old gray car, not American. That was the first thing I said when we were inside and moving: "This isn't an American car, is it?"

"It's a Volvo," said the girl I had spoken to at the counter. It was a two-door car, and we were crowded in, the six of us. I wondered why they agreed to take Sue and me along. They must have been a little crowded even before we joined up. The driver was the boy with the band around his head. We were moving, but I had the feeling he wasn't paying much attention to what was going on. He'd look out the side window. He'd sing to himself and then he'd laugh when there wasn't anything to laugh at. We were talking about the weather, and where we came from, stuff like that. He was smoking dope, I knew right away. I'd tried dope, but always with friends, in their rooms or mine, and never in a car. I wasn't really worried that the driver was smoking; I was more worried because he seemed strange. Sue stared at him as if her life depended on it, and maybe she was right to be so nervous but I knew it wouldn't do any good to sit there and worry. So I told her we should try to get some sleep and we leaned on each other and closed our eyes. The guy sitting on the other side of me was also trying to sleep.

I must have slept some, though I woke up still tired. For a second before I opened my eyes I thought I was back home in my room, listening to my favorite record. I used to have a boyfriend who loved the same records I did, and before we broke up that's all we did, listen to them. I thought of him, too. I thought of him and me, sitting and listening to records and smoking. We didn't use much pot, just a joint or two when we'd listen to records on the weekends.

Suddenly I was wide awake, and the car was moving, and I looked to see if there were other cars in front of us or behind us, but there were no lights in sight. It must be midnight, I thought, or even later. Only the driver was awake. I wanted to talk with him; I wanted to ask him where we were, how far from Chicago, but he seemed in his own world, and he looked a lot older than I had thought he was. I tried to go back to sleep. Then there was a lot of noise. A truck was bearing down on us. Our car veered, and I thought for sure we'd go off the road. But no, we kept going, and in a flash the truck was past us and gone, a speck of red light in the night way up the road.

"That was a big truck," I said without intending really to speak what was on my mind.

"They're all big," the driver said, and he turned around to look at me.

"Watch out!" I said, and I was surprised at how loud my own voice was.

"Watch out for *what?*" He looked ahead, then looked at me again, as if he was going to show me that no one could tell him what to do.

"Well, you never can tell when a truck's coming — until it's there, right on you."

"Is that so? Do you drive a lot, sister?"

"Sometimes. I don't have my license, but I can drive."

"The same with me. I've never bothered getting a license; they're stupid pieces of paper issued so the city or state can collect your money."

"What if a policeman stops us?"

"If he does, we're in trouble — whether I have a license or not. The police are out to beat us up."

"Not all the police are like that. I have a friend in school, and his father is a policeman, and . . ."

"You have a friend in *school,* and he's a *cop's boy.* That's nice to hear. The next thing we'll hear when we put on the radio is that there's a nationwide hunt for you. Then we'll get stopped at some road barrier and be arrested — all because we gave you a lift. Man, I should stop the car right now. I should let you out over there in that field. You could sleep there, and then in an hour or two the sun will be up, and some cop will come along and give you a ride."

"Knock it off," the boy beside me said. He was awake and listening. I looked at him. His eyes were closed and he seemed to be asleep, but his left knee was jerking up and down, and he held his hand up, palm out, as if he was trying to stop someone or hold up traffic while people crossed the street.

"Knock it off yourself," the driver said.

I wished I was asleep like Sue. I closed my eyes and tried to pretend I was asleep, but the two men began arguing about Sue and me — about whether

they should keep us in the car or tell us to get out —
and soon everyone was awake, Sue and the two girls
up front. Finally we all agreed that they'd let us off
at the next interchange, at an all-night diner just
off the Interstate. Then they'd go on to the place
where they didn't want us with them — resting, eat-
ing, sleeping. I was beginning to be afraid that we'd
have a hard time getting away from them. I never
thought I'd find myself afraid of hippies; I always
thought they were gentle people. But that driver
was almost as bad as my father. When I got out I
slammed the door and forgot to thank them. They
didn't say a word to us either, not one goodbye. They
probably had a ton of dope in that car, and that's
why they wanted to get rid of us. We might get them
in trouble, and they'd be arrested on a drug charge.

Sue and I were both stiff, but happy to be by ourselves. We stretched ourselves and joked about doing
some exercises. For a minute or so we said nothing to
each other. Then we argued. Sue said the driver was
just scared that the police would blame everything
on them if we got caught in their car.

"Why would the police be after us?" I asked her.

"Well, we're runaways."

"Come on, Sue. You're sounding like that driver, so doped-up I thought sure he'd run us off the road. Listen, neither your parents nor mine will call the police. They'll know we're safe, that we're just staying away from them."

"Sallie, let's call them, please let's. I don't want to argue with you, I just want to call my mother and tell her I'm O.K., and I'm on my way to Chicago, and I'll be back soon."

"Are you going to start that again? Let's get to Chicago first. Then we can call. If we call now, they *will* get the police after us."

We went inside the diner, which was warm, too warm, and full of smoke. There were five or six trucks outside, and the truck drivers sat, sipping on their coffee. When we came in everyone turned and stared at us. I began to wish we were in that old gray car, sleeping. Sue asked for a glass of milk as soon as we sat down at the counter, and the waitress smiled at us. "Sure you don't want beer, honey?"

"Come on, Helen, give her the milk," said the man sitting next to me. He was tall and thin, and he had on a green army jacket. I was sure he was a truck driver. He was smoking a cigarette and drinking coffee. An open newspaper lay beside him and he went back to reading it. The waitress asked Sue if she wanted anything else, and she said she wanted toast. I ordered coffee, black, and nothing else. The man spoke up again: "And hurry it up, Helen."

"Shut up, Jim. Mind your own business."

"I just want to make sure you do justice to all your customers!"

"Sallie, are you really going to drink that coffee without milk or sugar?" Sue asked.

Leave it to Sue, always ready to let air out of a balloon. All I was trying to do was show that waitress how tough at least *one* of us was — and now Sue was treating me as if I were a five-year-old.

"Yes, only I hope it's not *weak,* the coffee."

Sue leaned over and practically whispered in my ear: "Sallie, what's the matter with you? Have I done anything wrong?"

"No, Sue. You're just being your usual self, that's all."

The truck driver turned and looked at us. He must

have decided that we were whispering because we were afraid of the waitress, because he said in a loud voice: "Look, you girls, don't pay any attention to Helen over there. She's a nice kid. She's only been drinking coffee herself the last year or so."

The waitress ignored him and brought us our orders. I was thirsty, but the coffee was hot. I drank my glass of water, then I sipped the coffee, then I poured some water in the coffee cup, then I drank the whole cup of coffee in about half a minute. Sue stared at me all the while, and I guess the truck driver did, too.

"Helen, I want you to give this nice young lady another cup of coffee, black, and bring her some toast because it's almost morning and time for breakfast."

I wished he would leave us alone. Then he asked me where we were headed. I said Chicago.

"I don't blame you for pulling in here. It's bad driving — too wet. But it's going to stop raining soon, then we'll be all right. Drive slow, though — at least until the roads dry out a little."

"I'm not driving. I wish I was. We're hitchhiking, my friend and me."

"You *are!* Where did you say you're trying to go to?"

"Chicago. My cousin lives there, near the Loop."

"Oh? I was born in Chicago. My brother lives there. He's a big shot — or at least he thinks he is. He manages a supermarket on the West Side someplace, don't ask me where. I haven't been to Chicago in five years. I used to hear that Frank Sinatra singing 'Chicago, Chicago, a wonderful town,' and I'd say to myself: what does *he* know about Chicago? It's a big city, too big. I'm glad I live in Indianapolis."

Sue was leaning over, trying to listen. She was feeling left out and I didn't know what to do about it.

"I'll tell you what, miss. I can take you both almost to Indianapolis. That won't solve your problems, but it'll give you a big shove. You'll be there in the early afternoon, and then if you're lucky you can catch another ride or two and get to the big city by evening."

"Oh, that would be great!"

I trusted him. I don't know why, but I trusted him completely. But not Sue. She was digging her elbow into my ribs.

"Sallie, what did I hear you say?"

She was whispering, but I was afraid the man would overhear. I stepped on her right foot and felt my face getting flushed. I was angry at Sue and afraid we'd lose a good ride. Fortunately Sue shut up. She didn't say one single word. She just finished her milk and got up and walked over to the jukebox and looked at it and then stared out of the window at the trucks outside and the rain. I let her stand there alone while I asked the truck driver when he thought we'd be leaving. He said in a few minutes; he wanted to smoke one more cigarette. He started kidding his waitress friend, Helen, and it was then that I looked over at Sue and realized that she was crying. I got up and went over to her, and asked her what was the matter. She didn't say anything.

"Come on, Sue, let's go to the rest room."

We both washed up, not saying a word to each other. For a second I forgot Sue. I stared at the fluorescent lights, which gave off a blue color. There was the usual antiseptic smell — and a puddle of water on the floor. I reached for a paper towel, and noticed that only four or five were there, and gave one to Sue, and said at least we were lucky enough to be able to dry our hands, but still there was no answer from her. I thought it would cheer her up that we had a ride into Indiana, and that only left a couple hundred miles or so until Chicago. It didn't. I felt sick when I saw she was crying, so I put my arm around her and said: "Come on, let's get out of here and go for a walk."

"It's raining," she sobbed, and wiped at her eyes with the wet towel.

"Not very much anymore."

The ladies' room door banged shut behind us and Sue straightened. "I'm all right, Sallie, don't worry about me. I'd rather be home, that's all. I'm home-sick. I'm not as strong as you. And I'm scared — to sit way up there on one of those trucks. How do you know what that truck driver is like, *really* like?"

Thank God she was whispering. I was angry and

I whispered back: "He's a nice man, I can tell. Truck drivers are supposed to be the best drivers on the road — and they say they're good people."

"Look at the way he pushes that waitress around. And he's making a play for us — for *you*."

"Sue! What's the matter with you? I wish my father was as nice and thoughtful. You're letting your imagination run wild!"

I pulled her gently toward the door of the diner. We opened it, then closed it and we were standing outside, but under a small awning — so we weren't getting wet. Sue was still crying. She had to do it, I was beginning to understand. I stood there and I could feel her shaking. I was ready to start crying myself but I didn't want to go back home. I was feeling lost and alone there, outside that diner, and I was sure glad that Sue was with me, even if she made me feel weak every once in a while. Then the truck driver opened the door and said, "Ready?"

"I have to go back and pay the waitress."

"I've done that. Let's go!"

He walked toward his truck and I whispered to Sue: "Come on! We'll beel better in a few hours.

We'll be over half our way to Chicago, and it's going to be a nice day, the man said. He said his paper forecast warm and sunny weather."

I was relieved when Sue started walking toward the truck.

Getting in was like climbing onto a horse. Inside was like being in a building. Sitting high up there beside the driver while he moved the wheel and stepped on the clutch and shifted the gears and pressed the brakes and looked into his side mirrors, was like being inside a huge machine. It groaned and clicked and the driver was terrifyingly in control. After he took us out of the parking lot and off the side road and onto the Interstate he seemed to relax and he started talking with us: "This is the first time for you girls, right?"

"What?"

"The first time you've been on a truck like this one."

"Yes, sir."

"My name is Jim. Call me Jim. What's your names?"

"I'm Sallie, and she's Sue."

"I have two girls like you, only they're a little younger, both under ten. Do you have brothers and sisters?"

We talked about our families, and in between we just stared out at the road. It was like being on the roof of a building; we could look down at the road and the cars passing by and they seemed far away and small. There was a lot of noise to listen to, so you thought twice before talking. The truck driver wanted to talk, though — and I guess I did, too.

"See, it's getting light. I love driving this truck through the night, but I'm always glad to see the morning. When I'm home I can't sleep nights. I like to listen to the radio; we can pick up WWL, all the way from New Orleans. My wife's a night owl, too. She says she's come to realize that she either stays up with me — or we get a divorce. We send the girls off to school, then we both sleep. I can sleep like a bear in hibernation when the sun is out and it's noon; but when it's midnight I can't fall off to save my soul, even if I'm tired and lying right there in my nice, big, warm bed at home."

I told him I liked to stay up and play my records,

but my father wouldn't let me — he believes in "early to bed, early to rise," and all that stuff. Sue was feeling better, now that the sun was coming up, so at last she began to talk: "I get drowsy when it's past midnight — even when I'm at a dance or someplace like that and having myself a real good time. I don't know why it is, but I can almost feel the clock turning to twelve."

"Related to Cinderella?"

Both Sue and I smiled at his joke, and he began to ask us some of the children's riddles he'd picked up from his daughters — like, what has holes in it but holds water — a sponge — and why does the farmer call his pig "ink" — because it's always running out of a pen. I thought maybe the poor man was a little simple, but I remembered some riddles myself (I hadn't thought of them in years and years) and the truck driver got a good laugh out of them and the time went by fast. We could tell it was moving along toward midmorning when more and more cars showed up on the road.

"They're like mosquitoes. They whiz by, and you try to stay clear of them. I hate cars. When I'm home

I let my wife drive the car. I can't make the change from steering this to steering our car."

"Soon I'll be able to drive," I said.

"Oh, so you're not sixteen yet."

"No; almost though."

"Well, be careful, young lady. Traveling the way you and your friend are traveling isn't flying first class. You're at the mercy of God knows who — and it takes hours to get where you're going, so you may have to go in and out of ten cars before you're through. Take my advice: if you don't like the looks of a guy who stops for you, tell him no, you'd rather wait. Then move away from his car as fast as you can."

Sue nudged me. She was beginning to like the man more and more! I still liked him, but not his lectures, and we got one after another. Finally I spoke up: "Millions of kids hitchhike, and there's no sweat to it. They get where they're going, and they get there without meeting the kind of people you talk about."

"Listen, you don't know the half of it. You've lived a nice, quiet life. I know the road. I've seen these crazy, hippie kids, driving their Volkswagen buses with flowers all over them. Would you want to ride with people like that — out of their minds, drug addicts, thieves and murderers?"

"That's not fair. Have you ever really talked with them?"

"You think I've got nothing better to do? That'll be the day."

I decided not to ask him any more questions. He was beginning to sound as bad as my father. I stopped listening and as I sat there I pictured us ringing my cousin's doorbell, and her answering, and the two of us in her apartment. The truck driver put on his transistor radio, and soon we were listening to the midmorning news, and then came a talk show: the people phone in questions, and the man tries to answer them, and he talks with the people about their ideas — what's happening to the country. Things like that.

"It's time to stop and get something to eat. There's a good place a few miles ahead."

"It's only ten thirty, they just announced on the program."

He wasn't going to let me get away with that:

"We've been moving since five. If you're not hungry, you can stay here. I thought the hippies say you shouldn't go by the clock. You should eat according to what feels natural — something like that."

"I'm really hungry," said Sue.

We pulled into the parking space and when Sue and I got out we were stiff. My legs didn't want to hold me up after all the time we'd been packed in close together and jogged by the ride. Once we were inside the restaurant I realized how hungry I was. I devoured eggs and bacon and toast and hot chocolate. So did Sue. The truck driver had two orders of eggs, and wanted us to do the same, but we said no. He was thin, very thin — so I asked how come, since he sat all day and had such a big appetite.

"It's in my blood. No one's ever been fat in my family. I have to eat like a horse to keep myself from losing weight."

"Let us in on the secret," I said to him, even though I knew he didn't have a secret to reveal to us.

"Well, I don't know it myself. I think if you live right, your body keeps in good shape. Now look at those kids over there. Look how fat that girl is. Look at that kid with her, with the long hair and the pimply face. What kind of *man* is that?"

I felt myself getting red in the face. I reached for the water and drank it all up. I looked at the clock — a little after eleven. Then I asked him how much longer to Indianapolis.

"Oh, an hour, not more."

I wanted to go over and talk with the kids he was laughing at. They seemed a little older than Sue and me, and they reminded me of some of our friends. They weren't hippies. They were just kids. I figured they lived nearby and had a day off from school. Then Sue reminded me — I guess because she saw me glancing over toward the kids: "They must be on their vacation. Ours begins next week."

"Do you think they're still in high school? I think maybe they're in college."

"Sallie, you always exaggerate. You always make people older. If anything happens, you make it better or worse than it really is."

"Cut it out. *You're* exaggerating!"

The truck driver was listening — I thought he was busy eyeing the waitress — and he practically shouted at us: "They're not in school at all. They're road bums. They're running away from home. They don't know where to go, or why they're going."

He looked angry for a second, but then he talked as if he really felt sorry for the kids: "One minute they get on my nerves. I'll be driving, driving, driving — when all I want is to be at home with my wife and kids. Then I see them — overgrown children — with their posters and signs and thumbs out, and mostly I won't pick them up, but sometimes I do. They're all excited about someplace they're trying to get to — and meanwhile I can hear my own kids asking their mother when I'm going to get home. It's crazy, this world. But I suppose those kids — take the ones across the room — are all mixed up, and you have to feel sorry for them. They probably had a raw deal at home. Some parents are no good, and some kids are no good."

"You're right," Sue said. She was agreeing with *everything* he said, even when he contradicted himself. As we were getting ready to leave he saw me looking at the kids again.

"You'll see plenty like that before you get to Chicago!"

Sue quickly added, "I wish *you* were going to Chicago. Then we'd know we were going to get there before the night begins."

"Oh, don't worry, kid. I'll let you out at a good spot."

And he did. He took us to a place just beyond a gas station. It was at the junction of the Interstate and another main road, and he said we would have no trouble picking up a ride. As he pulled to the side of the road he pointed out the place we should stand — but he needn't have. Ten people were standing in a line, waiting for rides.

"See what I told you. Half of them are hippies; maybe all of them."

"Thank you," said Sue, as we climbed down. I thanked him, too.

"Take care of yourselves," was the last thing he said, and in a second the truck was inching away from us, noisier outside than it was inside.

WE WALKED toward the people standing there with signs. Some wanted local rides, some were going to Chicago or Milwaukee, and there were two signs that said CALIFORNIA. I nudged Sue and said, "Let's try California instead of Chicago." Her face suddenly looked as if it was falling apart.

"Come on, Sue." I tried to laugh. "Where's your sense of humor?"

"Sallie, sometimes I think you've left your head someplace — but I can't figure where."

"Well, Sue, I agree. Let's first get to Chicago — then we can argue about California."

We didn't know where to stand. As we approached the stretch where people were standing a car swerved over and I thought it was going to stop and pick up five or six people, because it was empty except for one man. Instead the man shouted something, and then drove away fast, gunning his engine and almost hitting some of the people standing there.

"Pig!" they shouted.

"What was that about?" Sue asked.

"I don't know. I think the man must have sworn at them, or something."

We came nearer and a girl said hello.

"Where you headed for?"

"Chicago."

"That won't be hard."

She seemed friendly, but she looked strange. She had on dungarees, with patches all over them. She had on a cape, and on it were messages: *Peace, Live and Let Live, Happiness*. She had on earrings almost as big as her face. She wore camping boots, like the kind my father wears when he goes hunting, only there were big holes in both, so all her toes were sticking out, all wrapped up in newspaper. The paper was torn and one of her big toes showed. Beside her was a boy who had hair as long as hers. He had on a big felt hat, not a cowboy hat, though — brown and still wet from the rain. He wore earrings, too. He had on cowboy boots and a leather jacket. He had a beard and a moustache. I had to look hard to figure out what he *did* look like, apart from the clothes and the hair. All I could make out were his blue eyes and a small nose, which he kept wiping with a red handkerchief.

"Chicago's a big city," he said.

"We're going to see my cousin," I answered.

"Why travel to see a relative?"

His girl friend whispered something to him; then he spoke to us: "I'm sorry, sisters. I shouldn't talk like that. I wish we had some cousins to go visit. My mother threw me out; her mother did the same to her. We'd like to go to New Zealand, but it's hard to hitch that far. We're going to try New Mexico, though. There are lots of nice people out there."

I didn't know what to say. Sue was standing beside me, closer than ever, and I knew she wasn't going to say anything. I began to look out at the highway, and wished that somehow we could get away from all the characters standing there, and get a ride from some truck driver like the one we'd just been with, or even a man like the one who first picked me up in his Cadillac. I could stand a lecture now, with only a few more hours to the Loop.

We just stood there. Cars came and went. I wanted

to get away from the people standing there; they all looked alike, and I could see that the people driving by didn't like what they saw — beards and dungarees and long hair on men, and beads and patches of bright colors or patches with messages on them. Sue pulled me, and this time I went along with her.

"Let's go up front. Let's stand by ourselves. These people are creepy."

"O.K."

We started walking past the others, but one of the men spoke to us: "You two planning to walk?"

I said no, just stand a little up ahead.

"We've been here before you. We take our turn."

"We don't want to go ahead of anyone; we just want to stand by ourselves. Some people are going to California; we're only going to Chicago."

"This isn't a marketplace or a stock exchange. We try to be fair to each other. We're all in this together. No one tries to get ahead."

I got angry. I wasn't trying to get ahead. All I wanted to do was get to Chicago. I didn't say anything, though. Sue and I stood there, up front — ahead of them all.

"They're not sisters," said a girl in granny glasses. "They're hoping to be secretaries or nurses or school-teachers — to be *used* by men."

I didn't know what she was talking about, but I felt very uncomfortable. She wore a long coat that almost touched the ground, and she was staring at Sue and me with an angry face. I didn't say anything. Her friend, a girl who had on an army jacket with part of the American flag sewn onto it, moved toward us: "You two don't know where it's at. We'd like to talk with you. Why don't you come to Milwaukee with us? We can put you up. We're going to a meeting there. You can join up."

I didn't answer her. For the first time I was scared. They were all looking at us, not the cars. I took Sue's arm and pulled her some more, until we were a few yards away from the rest of them.

Sue didn't know what to say. She just looked at me, and I whispered to her: "Don't talk with them. Don't look at them. Just look at the cars as they come near."

In a few seconds a Volkswagen bus pulled up. It had flowers on it, and there were two people inside, a man and a woman. They opened up the door and said they could take four, maybe five people. Five piled in, and I was glad. There were still five or six of them standing there, but our chances were better now, I figured. But then a car pulled up, an old station wagon, a Chevy I believe, and out came four more looking about like the others. They all started talking like old friends and Sue and I felt even more left out. We just stood there, holding our arms up, pointing our thumbs toward Chicago. Meanwhile they talked and laughed and passed reefers around and joked about the "poor people" who drove by in new American cars. "Man, I wouldn't take a ride from that big luxury ocean liner that just sailed by. If he gave me the car as a present, I'd give it back and say, Mister American, it's yours, all yours."

The guy's girlfriend had to put in her two cents: "I'd take it. I'd take it and drive it to a junkyard, and I'd get it compressed by one of those machines, and then I'd take the metal to a place where they make bird feeders or good toys for children or bicycles, something like that, and give them a present — a Buick, the compressed essence of a Buick!"

A second later another Buick came by. The man wanted to stop for Sue and me, I could see. He pulled toward us, but looked at the others, and then got frightened, I guess. Maybe he thought they would all come rushing toward his car. Maybe he thought we were part of them. Maybe he just panicked at the last moment. All I know is that Sue and I began to worry: "Sallie, we'll never get a ride."

"We've only been here a few minutes."

"A few minutes! It's been ten or fifteen minutes, at least."

"Sue, you *always* exaggerate."

"I'm a novice compared to you."

I didn't answer. I just stared at every driver, trying to get their eyes; I mean, I tried to lock eyes with them. I remembered hearing on a television program that some people can send messages to other people without saying a word. I kept repeating to myself: Stop, stop, stop your car and get Sue and me out of here.

Finally a car did stop. I really do think it was my way of looking at the driver. He had a Mercury, a green and tan one. His radio was going full blast when he pulled up; we could hear it even though his windows were almost completely shut. He swerved in fast, stopped his car with a jerk right in front of us, opened the door himself, and practically shouted at us. "Come on in, and shut the door before those lousy hippies get their paws on this new car."

For half a second I was paralyzed. I didn't know what to do or say. I didn't dare look at Sue; if I had, we'd have stood there and not said yes and not said no. I moved a foot or so. As I reached for the door, it occurred to me that I should ask him where he was going — but by then we were both in the car!

"What are two kids like you doing with a bunch like that?"

He had the car up to seventy or seventy-five by the time he'd asked us that question — and we were barely in the car and getting settled. His voice roared over the radio, which he did not turn down. He had a cigarette, the last inch of one, resting on the ashtray. He was well dressed, with wavy brown hair and gold cuff links. I was sure he was a traveling salesman.

I didn't know what to say. In my ears I could still hear what one of the hippies said as Sue and I got in: "Don't! That's no way to travel!"

"You both deaf?"

"No, I was trying to answer your question. We *weren't* with them. A truck driver left us there. It's a good place to get rides. That's why we were there, and that's why they were there."

"Well, that's good news. I saw you two, and I thought: a couple of pretty young girls, maybe out for a lark — but look at the company they're keeping! So, I thought I'd stop and save you, both of you — though I think you're the one who needs saving the worst."

He winked at me as he was talking, and I stared back. Sue sat there, silent as can be. I could tell that she didn't want to talk, not even with me. She just wanted the time to go as fast as possible. So, she stared out the window, stared at the houses that went by one after the other, stared at some cows grazing, some horses, stared at the cars we passed and the cars that wouldn't let us pass — even at eighty. I wished I could be like Sue; I wished I could turn away from that man and look and look and keep quiet. But even if I wanted to do that, he wouldn't let me. He began treating me like a girl friend or something; he began pointing out signs or automobiles or an occasional hitchhiker, and then he would tell me what this town was like, or that place, and how he once drove a Pontiac or a Dodge, and how he usually doesn't pick up hitchhikers but this time was different: "You're a nice-looking girl, pretty I'd say, so I thought I'd pull up and take you along. To tell you the truth, I thought for a minute you were with that pack of idiot kids, but then I saw it all: you wanted to break away from them, and I could help, so I did."

I didn't answer him. I hadn't liked him from moment one, but now I hated him. Poor Sue, she just sat there. The more he talked, the more she kept her head turned toward the right window of the car. I was in the middle, of course, and I found myself wishing I was sitting in the back — and wondering if it would be worth it to ask him to stop and let us *both* sit in the back, or else get out altogether. I didn't even know how far he was going.

"Are you going to Chicago?" I asked.

"Hell, no. I'm just going an hour or so up the pike. Then I turn off to sell more appliances, and then I'm free for the evening. I tell you, kid, it's too bad you're not alone. I could show you a good time."

I didn't say anything. I felt a little scared, now that he was talking like that, but I was also tired, and I thought the best thing would be for me and Sue to go right to sleep — and let him say anything he wanted. So, I told him I could barely keep my eyes open, because I'd been up all night, and I was afraid I might go off — so to be sure and wake me when it was time for us to get out.

"What kept you up all night, kiddo?"

"We were hitching."

"Running away from something — from *somebody?*"

"We're going to visit my cousin in Chicago."

Then I slumped back and over toward Sue and shut my eyes, and so did she. I pretended to be asleep. I breathed deep breaths, and spaced them out. At camp my girl friends used to snore, and that was when I knew they were in a *deep* sleep. Meanwhile, he fiddled with his radio, turning the sound up even higher, lighted another cigarette, and then mumbled to himself.

We did fall asleep, Sue and I. The next thing I knew the man was holding my arm, and I was screaming. I thought he was pulling me over to him, that's what I woke up thinking — and I wasn't sure we were in his car. I guess I thought for a second we were stopped someplace, and Sue was gone, and he was pulling me harder and harder and I was bending over, and —

"You two, hey you two, wake up! You want to see something, you want to see a real bad sight?"

The car *was* stopped, but up ahead other cars were also stopped. It was as if we were in a traffic jam in the middle of a city.

"There, over there, up ahead!"

I looked and saw it, a big truck overturned on the side of the road. It must have just happened, because there weren't too many cars ahead of us, and we were quite near the truck. No ambulance was there, but a man was lying on the bank of the road, and several people were standing over him.

"The fool — he must have fallen asleep at the wheel. Truck drivers are fools, most of them. They get huge amounts of money for steering those big things, and I hear a lot of them steal the cargoes they haul. He was probably drinking, too."

I didn't dare open my mouth. I wanted to hit him! I thought to myself that if I had my brother's baseball bat handy and could conk him hard and then leave. He was so nasty about everyone — and he was worse than everyone he criticized. As far as truck drivers go, if this guy sitting next to me was half as nice as our truck driver — well he'd be a half-decent person.

"We'll be here an hour. You wait and see. Why don't they let us by? They could keep a lane open. The police are as stupid as the truck driver."

"Maybe the police are more worried about the man who's hurt than about whether these cars get by." I wanted to say more, but he scared me — sitting there, puffing on his cigarette, hitting his steering wheel with both his hands and pushing his brakes up and down when we were already standing still.

I thought to myself, maybe now is the time to ask him if Sue and I can go in the back and try to sleep there. Of course, Sue and I were both wide awake and he could see it. Sue was afraid to open her mouth. Then he started getting pushy. He stretched. He leaned back. He poked my back with his hand.

"I'm sorry," he said — and he rubbed my back where he had poked it. Sue sat there frozen in her seat, and I strained toward her. She had her hand on the door ready to open it, and I guess I was leaning *too* far over toward her, because the man started laughing: "You two kids — that's all you are, a couple of little brats acting big. What are you afraid of? If you're scared, you should have thought twice before you started hitchhiking. What's a guy like me driving along on an Interstate supposed to think when he sees two girls standing there smiling at him with their thumbs out?"

"That we wanted a ride," I blurted out.

"Oh, yeah — you're sweet little babes in the woods, and you just want a nice feller to pick you up and take you to Chicago. Well, you look to me as though you've been around. Look at that bunch you were standing with, look at those fancy clothes you're wearing. You make me sick."

He made me sick and I was about to yell at Sue to get out when all of a sudden he yanked the key out of the ignition and opened the door.

"We may be here for half an hour before they get traffic moving again. I'm going to stretch my legs."

As soon as he left Sue started crying. She shook. She held her head in her hands and shook. I was ready to cry, too.

"Sallie, let's get out. Let's *walk* to Chicago. I don't like him — I don't trust him. I don't like the way he drives, *speeds*. I don't like his looks. I don't like the way he dangles his cigarette out of the corner of his mouth. I don't like the way he talks."

"Sue, we want to get to Chicago, right? We can afford to humor him. He won't bother us. He's just a lot of talk."

"He's no good."

I saw him up ahead, talking to someone, leaning on a car — and I hated him.

"O.K., let's get out right now."

"Do you think he'll chase after us when he sees us walking away from his car?"

"Sue! We're not prisoners. We have a right to go anywhere we please. We can walk on the side of the highway. If he bothers us, we can call the police."

"What if he starts *chasing* us; what if he's *after* us? And if we did get to a policeman — he'd want to know what *we're* doing here on this road, wouldn't he?"

"There's nothing wrong with hitchhiking. Millions of kids do it."

"Maybe you're right but we have no identification, nothing. My father always shouts at my brother to carry his wallet around, so he can show his social security number if he gets stopped, or his driver's license."

"Well, we haven't got any. We're not old enough."

"That's the point; the policeman would want to know where we come from, and he'd call our parents — and they'd say hold them there, both of them, or send them home."

"I wouldn't mind getting a ride from a policeman, if he'd take us to Chicago. Maybe we could call my cousin and tell her we're going to pretend she's our mother, and then turn ourselves in to the police and tell *them* we're lost, and could they call her, and help us get back to her!"

"Sallie, you're losing your mind."

By now Sue had stopped crying. Maybe we were both going nuts. I sat there in that big car, looking at the blue leather seats and the cigarette butts in the ashtray and the box of samples, jewelry samples, the salesman had on the floor, and I looked at the clock, telling us it was near noon, and I wondered what was going on at home, and at school — and I had to pinch myself to make sure this wasn't some crazy dream. Then I decided we had to use our heads.

"Come on, Sue, let's get out, right now."

"Now?"

"Now or never. He'll be back soon."

She opened the door and was out on the road. I was right behind her. I slammed the door so hard I was sure the guy would hear it and come running. For a second I had an idea: why not let the air out of his tires, all four of them? Then what could he do? But he might try to find us and have us arrested, and the best thing, I figured, was go off to the side of the road and walk away and hide, and when the cars get moving, come back and start hitching again.

Sue started up the road toward the truck. I called her back.

"Let's go off toward that field. See the trees there, we can hide for a few minutes — and rest, too."

"What if they see us?"

"Sue, what if *who* sees us? I think we're both wacky. We're behaving as if we're both freaked out. Maybe we shouldn't go running off to hide. Maybe that man would be glad to get rid of us. I don't think he likes us any more than we like him. I'll bet he's a gambler. He works for some gang or something!"

"Sallie, it's *you* who's going off your rocker. That man wouldn't last for a minute in any gang. He talks about himself too much."

"Well, you're right. Besides, he's a coward. I'm sure he is. If I kicked him and bit him he'd probably run and plead for mercy."

"Sallie!"

"Well, I just want you to know that *we've* got some cards, too; we don't have to sit around wondering what *he'll* do. That's like being at home. Will Daddy say yes or will he say no? What will mother ask me to do now, and *then* what will she want? That kind of thing."

"I wish I were home now, even with the problems I have with my folks."

"Well, maybe. But what *do* we do right now? What's our next step?"

"Sallie, you got us into this. You decide. I give up figuring out what comes next. I never dreamed yesterday morning I'd be out here, wherever we are, and I hope and pray we'll be home tomorrow morning. *There* — I've been honest!"

"O.K. Let's walk a little ahead."

We passed one car, then another. Most of the cars were empty. There was a crowd up near the truck and a police car was there with its blue light going around and around, and an ambulance, too. I wanted to be right there, seeing what there was to see, and so did Sue. We'd walked very fast at first, but now that we were a car or two away from the scene of the accident we both stopped.

"I don't think we should go any nearer, Sallie."

"No one will notice us. You know, Sue, the whole world doesn't turn on every move we make."

"You've stopped walking; you slowed down a few seconds ago, just when I did."

"I'd like to get a new ride, that's what I'm after."

I turned away from Sue and looked back at the cars we'd passed.

"Let's walk back along the side of the road. We'll ask someone for a ride."

WE MOVED from car to car. There were three rows of them, and we kept to the inside. Two boys in a sports car said hello and seemed friendly and very nice, not too much older than us, and like us — I mean, they could have been any one of twenty-five boys I knew at high school, only a year or two, maybe three years older. But their car only had the two seats they were in — it was a foreign car — so there was no use stopping and talking with them. There was a man resting his head on the steering wheel of a pickup truck, and I almost suggested to Sue that we climb on up and sit in the back. That way the man wouldn't even know we were there, and we could sit and talk to each other, Sue and me. But we'd have no idea where he was headed, and we both were hoping for a regular car ride, not another shaking up in a truck. Besides, the man looked as if he was really fast asleep, so he must have been tired — and with the straw hat on, I was sure he was a farmer, only going a short way up the road. Then we came to a red Mustang. The young man sitting in it was whistling to himself. He smiled and I smiled, and he spoke out through his half-open window: "How's it going? Another hour or another minute or two?"

"Another few minutes, I believe."

"Good. I'd like to get going."

I almost asked him if he'd take us, but I couldn't find the words. Both Sue and I hesitated, but we moved on. We looked at each other and thought the same thing: he seemed nice. But we kept on, and passed cars filled with families and a telephone company truck and a bigger truck and a Volkswagen bus again, one of those with flowers on it and some guys smoking away and laughing. And then the end of the cars, and the open highway and more cars coming up — more and more, until you wonder if there's ever a time on a highway like this when there are no cars to be seen, when people are all off home asleep or at work or in church or something.

We turned around and I couldn't get that red Mustang out of my mind, and Sue couldn't either, because she immediately spoke up: "Maybe we should go talk to that man in the red car, the Mustang."

"Good idea."

I was afraid that all of a sudden the traffic would get going, and in a few seconds the cars would be gone, every one of them, and there we'd be, Sue and I, on that wide open stretch of highway. And then the police might come by and pick us up and question us. But the cars stood still, and in a minute or two, it seemed like, we were standing in back of the red Mustang — wondering what to do next, what to say.

"Hey, you two. Coming back from a walk? I should get out and take a walk myself."

He'd seen us through his rearview mirror, I guess. Sue smiled, and so did I. We stood still for a second or two, then I walked up to his window, and there he was, smiling as he was before. "I think the cars will be moving soon, so there's no time for walking," I said. "We're looking for a ride; that's why we've been walking. Would you mind — could we please ride with you?"

"Oh, I didn't realize, or I would have . . . Yes, sure." And he leaned over to open the door on the other side.

We scooted around the front of the car so fast that we were there the same time his hand reached the door. Sue got in the back, and I was going to go in the back with her, but the man seemed friendly, and it seemed rude for both of us to be in the back, so I sat down in the bucket seat up front — and immediately felt sorry for Sue, sitting all hemmed in back there while I had so much room.

"Would you like to hear some music while we wait? I have the radio, or some tapes."

"Oh, that's fine. Whatever you wish, that's fine."

I sat there and began to relax. I thought to myself: he's polite, he's nice. He switched on the radio, and there was some country rock, and he seemed to like it, and Sue and I looked at each other and sent messages saying, this guy's a gift from heaven. In a few minutes cars started moving, and finally we were on our way. The man offered us each a cigarette, told us we were lucky we didn't smoke, got his cigarette going, opened the window a little more, stretched himself as he accelerated the car, and finally broke the silence, after turning the radio down a little: "Where you going?"

"To Chicago, to visit my cousin."

"I like Chicago. Wish I could take you right to where you're going; and if it were some other time I probably could, because I often go there. But I'm stopping near the dunes just before the Illinois state line, so I'll have to leave you off there. It's only about an hour from there into the city, depending on the traffic."

I could have shouted or cried, I was so happy. Sue said it all in one big, loud, "Wonderful!"

Then he introduced himself, as if we were meeting at a party or something: "I'm Jack Lawson, and I teach at De Pauw University. Political science."

"I'm Sallie, and she's Sue."

"Are you both working, or do you go to school?"

I guess he thought we were older. I told him we went to school, that we were on vacation and visiting my cousin. It turned out *he* was on vacation, too. Then I asked him where De Pauw was and he laughed and said there was no reason I should know, and it was in Greencastle. I didn't know what state Greencastle was in, and he said one thing he knew for sure, I wasn't from Indiana, because the chances are a kid from Indiana would know that De Pauw University is in Greencastle, and that's just west of Indianapolis.

"Do you want to go to college?"

"I don't know."

Then he asked if our parents wanted us to go to college, and I said my parents just wanted me to obey whatever rules they had, and they hadn't said yet whether going to college was on their list of things we had to do, period. He smiled and said something that scared me a little — though he wasn't sounding suspicious when he spoke: "You sound as if you're running away from home."

I didn't answer. Sue didn't, either. But he saw me turn and look at Sue and he heard our silence.

"You *are* running away from home."

"No, we're not," said Sue.

"We're going to my cousin's," I said, "and our parents don't know it now, but we'll phone them when we get there, and they'll be glad."

"How long have you been on the road?"

I'd forgotten. It seemed like a month or a year, not an afternoon and a whole night and half a day. I was trying to settle in my own mind how long it had been when he glanced toward me and gave a quick look back at Sue and then said, "I'd say two or three days."

"How do you know?" I said.

"Well, you both look tired and your clothes are wrinkled and your hair is a little straggly, but you're not really dirty and worn down, the way I've seen kids look who've been hitching across the country."

"You'd make a good detective," Sue said.

"Are any detectives after you?"

"I doubt it. Sallie's mother probably called my

mother when Sallie didn't come home, and they must have decided we were hiding someplace. A year ago we hid in a friend's house overnight. Her parents were away. Then the next day we found that our parents didn't even call the police. I think another friend of ours told our parents, though. They must have thought we did the same thing last night — but I'm sure they're worried by now."

"Hadn't you better call them, then?"

"Sallie will call, when she's at her cousin's."

"But that's hours away. Even with luck you won't be in Chicago until tonight, maybe *late* tonight."

I got annoyed at the two of them; back and forth, back and forth they went, with all that talk about my parents and Sue's parents. For a second I pictured my mother crying, and I could feel the tears in me. But I reminded myself that my mother is a doormat to my father. My poor mother. I don't care how much Dad worries about me — the more the better! Fortunately the man stopped talking. He told us he was tired, and he had all he could do to keep his eyes open, so he didn't want to talk, just drive. I worried that he'd fall asleep and we'd crash and get killed —

we were going at sixty, slow for that highway, but pretty fast when a driver falls asleep. I kept looking at him, but his eyes were wide open and he didn't even look tired.

I was tired myself. I dozed on and off as we moved up the road, past farms and farm roads and parallel roads with motels and gas stations on them, in sight but far away, because you really have to work to get off an interstate. I never really fell asleep, though. Sue seemed asleep every time I looked over at her, and I envied her — stretched out on that back seat. My head bobbed and I had all kinds of thoughts: my mother crying again, my father making the noise he always does, my cousin being surprised when we get there, and kissing me and cooking us a big supper, the truck driver we'd gone with during the night, and now this man. I pictured him teaching political science to a room full of students, though I wasn't even sure what political science was. Once I decided that he was worried — not only about us but himself: we're running away from home, and maybe the police have been called, so he might get in trouble for giving us a ride.

Anyway, time went fast. The sun was over toward the west and I could feel my stomach shouting how hungry it was. Why doesn't he stop for something to eat, I kept wondering. Maybe he had an early lunch, before that accident. Finally I heard him telling us to wake up, and I realized I must have been at least a little asleep, and I thought, he's going to stop now, and we could get an ice cream cone or something — but he surprised us: "I'll be stopping soon to let you two off and take another road. You'd better wake up."

I did, and Sue half-did. I reached over and shook her a couple of times and finally she sat up and pushed her hair out of her face. She yawned and said, "Sallie, we *must* be near Chicago, we just *must* be."

The man told her not to worry: "You're a lot nearer than you were a few hours ago," and he pulled to the side of the road.

"This is probably the best place to get out. Up ahead is a turnoff — and a good place for cars to stop and pick you up. You're still in Indiana, but Illinois is only a few miles ahead. The dunes and Lake Michigan are nearby; it's a warm day, and I think you girls would enjoy a good swim. Anyway, good luck to both of you!"

We thanked him and a minute later we were standing on the side of the road again, all by ourselves, cars whizzing by and no one paying any attention to us. I had no watch, and Sue didn't either, but it seemed like hours we were there. I began to hate those cars that passed us. I'd watch each car, and say to myself no, he's not going to stop, and I'd let go at the driver in my mind with words my father thinks he's the only one who has a right to use.

We were in the worst possible place. The cars were going very fast, there were just the two of us, and no cars at all were coming onto the Interstate. That college professor didn't know his roads. There was only an exit where he'd let us out, not an entrance, too — as he said there was when he said goodbye and told us to walk up a few yards ahead and "catch a car entering."

I even found myself thinking back to the time we had with the salesman; he was a real pain, and full of himself, but he was savvy as they come, and I decided that if he had let us out someplace, he would have known where he was putting us and what our chances of getting a ride were. Then it started getting dark. Sue and I were getting jumpy. Would we have to spend the night near the road — or get picked up by a police car? Should we walk into the nearest town? Should we, maybe, try to go to the dunes and swim a little and sleep there on the sand? We were lucky, because it actually was warm enough to do that! We got angrier and angrier at the professor — for leaving us in a place that turned out to be the worst one we'd been in. As Sue put it, "he really could have put himself just a little out of the way for us. The truck driver did."

For a few minutes I began to wish the police *would* come. I pictured myself sitting in the back of their car, the sirens going, the light on the roof whirling around — and all the cars that had just passed us being made to move over and slow down.

Boom, boom, boom they continued to come, the sound hitting you in the face, slapping you, almost pushing you over. "Rat!" I yelled at a yellow convertible. "Rat!" I yelled at a blue four-door sedan.

"Stop it, Sallie."

"Why? I'd like to grab them and ask them why they can't make room in their fancy cars for a couple of people trying to go someplace. That professor — he could have taken us near enough to the city so we could get a bus ride."

"Leave him alone. Forget him. You're just dumping on him, Sallie."

"Do you look forward to staying here all night? If you like that professor so much, why don't you call up his college and find out where he lives and have him come back, come back right now, and help us!"

He's going to visit someone, so he's not home — otherwise I *would* do it. I'd do just what you suggest, and I'll bet he'd come, too. He's a gentleman."

"I'll take the truck driver any day."

"You can have the truck driver."

"You can have that professor and his lousy car."

Sue walked away from me. She kept on walking and then she started hitching — as if she was on her own and not with me. The cars that sped by me sped by her, too — but I began to worry that one of them would pass me and stop for her. She was smiling at them, and then she started waving at them — and when I motioned to her to come back, she stuck out her tongue at me and shouted that I was a freak. Then like idiots we both began to cry, and we fell into each other's arms and we just stood there beside the highway holding onto each other and saying we were sorry and saying we were tired and we wished we were in Chicago, or we wished we were home — anywhere but where we were.

THEN THE TWO motorcycles appeared, small black dots at first, then the white helmets, and they got bigger and bigger, and then the noise, and suddenly we were sandwiched in between them: "Hey, why are you standing here? Get on."

We stood there, speechless and not even sure at first that we both hadn't, at last, started having nightmares.

"What do you want, engraved invitations? Tell us where you want to go and we'll get you there."

That was too much for me to resist: "You *will?*

96

Well, we want to go to Chicago, that's where we want to go."

"You don't say!"

One repeated what the other said, and meanwhile Sue and I didn't know whether to say yes and leap on, or say no, and ask them to go away and leave us alone. We just stared at those big leather seats, and the wheels, the wires, the speedometer, the chains with the locks.

"Look, we can't take you to Chicago," the one to my left said, "but we can take you to the dunes. There are a lot of people from Chicago who have summer places there, hideaways, cottages they go to, even in the middle of the week. They send electricians and carpenters and plumbers out there to do work around this time of year. We can take you there, and you can rest up and take a swim and get some sleep and tomorrow you can get a ride easy, real easy, to Chicago."

I wanted to say O.K. and go along with him, but I knew Sue was frightened, and I was, too. I thought to myself that maybe we should stay right where we were a little longer, and hope someone would see us and say, Look, I'm going to Chicago, where are you going? But the cars were putting on their lights and they were going by at sixty and seventy and eighty, and I was sure, as I stood there and thought about it for a second or two, while those guys raced their engines, and took off their helmets and put them back on again and kicked a few rocks with their feet — I was sure that we'd either have to go with them or try to find a place to sleep in some field.

"Sue, let's go with them. We'll feel better near the water. They say the dunes are practically a suburb of Chicago; and even if they're not, I think we've got to stop now. I don't think we'll catch a ride from this place — not even tomorrow in broad daylight. Let's go with them. It'll be good to get off the road."

She didn't say anything. She nodded her head and smiled weakly and was on one of the motorcycles before I had a chance to get on the other one — and off we went! I had never been on a real, big, black motorcycle before, only on small motorbikes. A boy I like at school has been trying to get a motorcycle for a year or so, but his father and mother say no, it's a ticket to death, they tell him. In my mind I heard him telling me that as we went along — fast as can be. And you really do go fast, and you really feel yourself moving. In a big car you don't realize how much territory you're covering, but on a motorcycle you feel as if you're going from coast to coast in five minutes.

The guy had told me to bury my head in his back and hold on to him, but I guess I'd looked out ahead too much, because my face began to hurt, as if I'd been sunburned. It was funny, holding on to this stranger, smelling the leather of his jacket and feeling his hair on my forehead. In the cars I minded it if one of the drivers leaned a little too heavily on me, but now I was holding on to this guy for all I was worth. When the road curved I squeezed him tighter, and once he said, "That's the way, kid."

It didn't take long for us to reach the dunes. We'd left the Interstate and were on a fairly narrow and deserted road, and soon we switched to an even narrower road, and soon there was no road at all, just sand, hills and hills of it — and the water of

Lake Michigan and a moon there, and then the moon gone in a second because of the clouds. I was tired in my bones, but all keyed up in my head because of that motorcycle ride. When we stopped I dropped my arms and sort of hung there on the seat. I couldn't believe I was alive and the ride was over. My head was still pushed against his leather jacket. I felt him say, "Why don't we all swim and get rid of the road dust."

I stumbled off and onto the sand. The other motorcycle had pulled up beside us. Sue sat glued to the seat, her hair and clothes plastered to her. She crawled off and we both tried to smile. Poor Sue, I thought; her hair looked terrible and she seemed even more exhausted than me. She didn't say a word. She stretched and stared at the water, and then up at the sky, and then at the motorcycle I'd been on. I didn't know what to say about going for a swim, but the guy didn't push us. He went right to work checking his motorcycle and so did his friend. I suddenly felt very stupid. Why did we let them bring us here? What would they try to do to us? What should we do, or try to do? I couldn't answer my own questions, and

I was afraid that any second Sue would start asking them. If she cried I couldn't stand it.

Finally I said something, and I couldn't believe it was me, talking so cool to Sue. "Let's go over there and sit in the sand."

"O.K."

I had pointed to a dune nearby and as we walked I turned around twice — and the two of them were busy working on their motorcycles. But not completely busy, because the one I rode with lifted his head up and shouted to us: "You need the rest. We do, too. We'll be right over."

"Sallie, let's run!"

"We can't. They'll come after us."

"Then, we can hide someplace."

"Where?"

"Look at all the dunes here. We could hide behind one of them. We could cover ourselves under sand."

"Sue, stop it! They haven't bothered us. They've been very nice to us. What's happened to you and me? Two guys come by on a motorcycle and offer to get us off the highway where we've been standing and no one's stopped, and they take us to a nice beach and tell us to go for a swim and rest, and they don't lift a finger to bother us — and we're scared to death. They seem like college kids. I don't know; maybe they work in a factory. They seem nice, that's all I can say."

"You might have to change your mind, Sallie. Look at those chains on their motorcycles. They could come after us with them."

"Look, we're here. If we run, we have no chance. We would only make fools of ourselves — I mean, suppose they really only want to talk with us and take care of their motorcycles and have a ride and go home."

Sue didn't answer — and I didn't blame her. I didn't believe my own words. We sat and let ourselves sink a little into the sand. It felt good there, soft and quiet. The air was still and warm. There were no mosquitoes — too early in the season, I guess. I took off my shoes and stretched out. The sand felt warm, and I dug my feet farther and farther into it. As my head hit the sand I felt more tired than I'd ever felt in my life. I felt myself going to sleep, and I fought and fought to keep awake. Sue stretched out in the sand, too, right beside me. We didn't talk. There was no use going over the same subject again and again. We could hear the guys talking, but only the sound, not the words. They seemed farther and farther away from us. I looked up at the sky. The moon seemed to have won: the clouds were gone. Sue's eyes were fluttering — open, then closed, then open, then closed. I remember thinking to myself that we could take a little nap, then ask the guys to drive us to a diner, and we could get some coffee there, and ask if anyone was going to Chicago. I might even call my cousin from the diner, now that we were so near the city. Then complete darkness and that last thought — how wonderful and suddenly very special it felt to be slipping off to sleep, even for a few minutes, and not in a car but here, on the ground, where everything seemed to be resting.

I felt Sue stir beside me. She was still asleep. I wasn't sure I wasn't asleep myself. I felt tired, groggy, unable to lift my legs or arms. I had a headache. I hadn't opened my eyes, but I felt the light out there beyond my eyelids. What had happened? Where were we?

"Sue!" The word came to my lips, but I wasn't sure I said it aloud. I did open my eyes, and sure enough, it was morning. The sun was coming up. The lake was there, and the sand, lots and lots of it, was still there. We hadn't moved, I began to realize, just gone into a deep sleep. The motorcycles, the two men — where were they? I looked. I remembered where they had been. I looked again. Gone! They must have left. There was no one in sight.

"Sue!" This time I spoke aloud. "Sue!" Now I shouted. Then I started pushing her, and she moved, and then she woke up. For a second she was like me, lost in trying to figure out where she was and what might have gone on and what to expect when she opened her eyes. Then she did. "Hi," she said, and I couldn't help laughing. "Sallie! What happened?"

"Nothing. I guess we fell asleep, that's all. It's morning."

"Where ... where are ..."

They've gone. I mean, I can't see them."

I decided to stand up. Maybe they *weren't* gone! Maybe they were nearby. But with the new view I got from my wobbly legs I still couldn't see them.

"They *are* gone," I told Sue, and she smiled. Then I began to panic. "Now we're really stuck. We were real unfair to those guys. They just wanted some company. They might have even taken us to Chicago if we'd stayed awake."

"What do we do, Sallie?"

Sue finally got herself up, too, as she asked me that. She looked around, to make sure for herself that I wasn't wrong, and then she started toward the water.

"Let's get our feet wet. We can't swim, but let's wade, and wash our hands and faces. The water looks clean."

"Why can't we swim?"

"What if . . ."

"No one is here. It's very early in the morning. If we can't see anybody, nobody can see us."

So we went for a swim, and came back and sat against a dune and dried out and got dressed — and felt brand-new. I was singing songs to myself. I was sure we'd be in my cousin's apartment in a couple of hours. We started walking down the road and there wasn't a car to be seen coming in either direction.

"We may have to walk to Chicago, Sallie."

"If we do, it'll only be another day or two. We're *almost* within walking distance now. Well . . . not really. But don't worry, we'll get a ride."

We didn't and we didn't; and we got tired all over again. We walked for four hours at least. At last we were away from the dunes and at the outskirts of a small town. We saw a bowling alley and a drugstore and a grocery store. We decided to try the bowling alley; maybe there would be some friendly people our own age and we could ask them if they knew anyone going to Chicago. We went inside and they had just opened and it was good to hear those familiar sounds again — the balls rolling, the pins falling, the shouts of someone who has made a strike or hit nothing at all. We stood there, behind some girls, and they smiled and one of them offered us some potato chips and we got to talking. No, we told them, we're not from around here and yes, we are passing through. One of the girls, the tallest, asked us where we were headed, and I said Chicago, and she said her aunt lives there, and I said so did my cousin, and she's the one we want to see.

"I can take you a few miles toward the city. I can at least get you into Illinois."

Of course we said yes, and thanked her, and were glad she didn't tell us we had to sit through a few more bowling games. She had lost, and she had no more money. Her friend offered to stake her to a game and take an I.O.U. — but no, she wanted to leave. So, we went with her and soon were driving along in her mother's 1965 (she told us) Chevrolet station wagon, black on the outside with blue leather seats.

ABOUT A MILE or so on the road toward the Interstate she picked up a friend of hers, a boy — who insisted he could sit with us up front, crowded as it would be with four. Sue and I both offered to go into the back, and even tried to get out, but the girl and her boyfriend wouldn't let us move. So there we all were, crowded together, while the back seat and the space behind it were empty. I didn't mind being squeezed, but I did mind the boy's tongue. He swore and made fresh remarks at us, and his girl-friend was as annoyed with him as we were: "You can get out right now if you don't stop — shut up."

"She's always talking like that to me. That's why we split up. I told her: you're as bad as Miss Pickles."

"Who is Miss Pickles?" Sue asked.

He answered: "She's a teacher who screams at you when she's in a *good* mood and goes nuts when she doesn't like you."

Then he started really bothering us — asking one question after another, squeezing against Sue and grabbing around her at my shoulder, suggesting that "we" (him and Sue and me) take over the car and ditch his girlfriend (he called her "my ex"). She got angrier and angrier at him — and kept apologizing to us for his behavior. Sue and I had come a long way since we'd left home, but the half hour or so we spent in that car was the worst time. Once I thought the girl was going to get into a fight with the guy — while she was driving. She took one hand off the steering wheel and threatened him, then she took the other one off and punched at him, almost hitting Sue. I grabbed the wheel.

"Don't worry, honey, I know what I'm doing," the girl said.

"Yes, don't worry, girls, she'll get you someplace, dead or alive!"

Then he shut up, and so did she, and I was afraid to break the silence with the question I kept wanting to ask: when do we get left off? As it turned out I didn't have to ask that question. Suddenly the car started to wobble. She held on to the steering wheel and took her foot off the gas pedal and put it on the brakes — and as we all watched her and felt the car shake, we heard a noise: a tire flapping under us.

"Your one hundredth flat tire. You two kids didn't know why she picked you up, did you? Now you know why she picked me up. Here we are again. She must have arranged it with the tires in advance. Just about every time she gets a flat, I'm aboard. This is a perfect example, right now!"

He hit at the door handle and was out. Sue followed, then me. The girl just sat there. He got down and looked at the tire — the front one on the right — and we walked over to the girl: "I'm sorry; I apologize to you two for the way he talks. He isn't as bad as he sounds. He didn't tell you that the first year, last year, the car was in his name, and he drove it most of the time. Sometimes I believe he makes slow leaks in those tires, then comes along — just so he can remind me that he's a man and I'm a woman and he knows how to fix flats and I don't."

I was amused by the two of them, they were growing on me. I wanted to tell her that we'd had a good time riding with them, but I wasn't sure they'd meant to give us a good time. They were funny without trying to be. He was whistling and singing while he got the jack and set it up, and every once in a while he'd crack a joke at his "ex's" expense. I felt we should stay there and try to cheer her up and help. As he put the bolts down on the ground I wanted at least to pick them up and hold them and be ready to hand them over, like I remembered doing once for my dad when I was much younger and we had a flat only a couple of blocks from our house. But I thought of my cousin again. I really did want to get to Chicago. We'd already crossed into Illinois, and I knew we weren't too far from a bus stop, where we could catch a bus to the Loop. So I got up my courage and spoke: "Would you mind if . . . I mean, my cousin is expecting us, and . . ."

The guy stood up: "Go ahead. Don't worry about us. That's what hitchhiking is all about. Just because someone picks you up, doesn't mean you have to promise to love, honor and obey, fix their flats, bail them out of jail, and help bring up their kids! Hitching is saying hello and traveling a way and saying goodbye!"

The girl was giggling by this time, and I figured she wouldn't mind if we left. As we walked away, the two of them stood there on the side of the road, near the flat tire, with the station wagon all jacked up and creaking a little.

"About a half a mile ahead, you'll find a bus stop," he yelled after us. "You can catch a bus into Chicago, or hitch in, if you haven't had enough of it."

We waved our thanks and continued walking. "They're funny," I said to Sue.

"I guess they are. I guess we are, too."

"Everyone is, if you get to know them."

"Right."

We got to the bus stop, and once there, it seemed stupid, to stand and wait for a bus, when all those cars were going by.

"Let's hitch," I said to Sue.

"Why? Haven't we done enough of that?"

"We're wasting time; we could be riding into the city with someone."

"Haven't you had enough of that, Sallie? I think you've become an addict — you can't travel the way others do. Instead you have to stick out your thumb, even when you can catch a bus and not run the risk of being picked up by God knows who."

"What do you mean, 'God knows who'?"

"Well, would you want to ride again with that gangster with the cigarette hanging out of the corner of his mouth?"

"Oh, *him!* Well, he was just one, one out of . . . how many?"

"I can't remember. But let's try a bus driver next. Maybe he'll be interesting, too!"

In a few minutes the bus came along. We had to give the driver a good stiff fare — it cost us more to travel those last few miles than the whole trip had cost — and he didn't say a word to us, no thank you, no smile, just a glare. When we were seated, Sue giggled and said: "You're right, a car is better; you can ride free and if you're lucky, listening to the driver is as good as watching TV."

The filling stations and motels came closer together and the buildings became taller, and there were people on the streets. We were in Chicago. We'd been in cities before, but never alone. We didn't know how to find my cousin's place, and when I finally got up courage to ask the bus driver he growled out: "How should I know?" I went back to my seat and said to Sue: "Let's get off, right now."

"Why? Are we near your cousin's?"

"No. He doesn't know where her street is."

"Then maybe we should stay on the bus. Maybe we'll be getting off too soon if we do it now."

"But we'll *never* know when to get off, if we just sit here. The driver isn't going to help us — even if he knew, he probably wouldn't tell us. Look at that face of his. Let's get off and find a policeman."

The next stop was at a crowded intersection, but

there was no policeman in sight. We were both standing at the door and the driver let us out. As we hit the curb I spotted a cab.

"Let's go ask the cab driver."

"Sallie, we might not be able to afford the cab. Let's go into a store — there, that drugstore."

"No. A cab driver is more likely to know, especially if we're far away from my cousin's. The druggist would only know the places nearby. We don't have to *take* the cab, just talk to the man."

I ran over, afraid he'd suddenly pull away. But the man was just sitting there half asleep, listening to the radio news.

"Sir. Mister."

"Yeah? Hop in."

"Well. We don't really want a ride. We were wondering . . . I mean, where is . . ."

For a second I forgot the exact address; then I remembered, and told him, and he said: "You don't need a cab, sister. Just walk up this street four blocks, catch a streetcar. Four or five stops and you'll be there. Ask the conductor."

We did what he said, and after we paid the fare

we were nearly broke. When we saw the apartment house, with the right number, the two of us stopped and just looked at each other.

"We're here, Sue."

"Yes, Sallie, we're here."

We went inside and looked for my cousin's name. I pressed the button beside it so long that Sue told me to stop. We waited, but there was no answer. I tried the door, and it was locked. I pressed the button again — and still no answer.

"She's not home."

"Of course she's not home, Sue. What's the matter with us! She's at work."

"What do we do now?"

"I don't know. Maybe we should go for a walk."

"We could go downtown and look at the stores."

"Are you kidding? I'm tired. I've had enough walking for a while."

We sat down in the hall, right under the buzzer. We were afraid that people would see us and call the police, but not so afraid that we didn't doze.

We both must have been sleeping, because the next thing I felt was some one push at me. A man was leaning over demanding, "What are you doing here? Go home and go to bed."

"We're waiting for my cousin. She lives here."

"Who's your cousin?"

"Miss Collins," I told him, and he knew her.

"She comes home in the midafternoon. You can't sleep here, though, not in the hallway. I'm the superintendent, and I can't allow it. I could let you into her apartment, but I have no right to. You go on down to the cafeteria; it's two blocks that way. You can sit there and no one will bother you. Just get a Coke or something."

We spent our last money on Cokes, and came back and tried that bell again — and this time, we got a reply. Sue and I flew up the stairs and we hit her landing and her door was open, and we all fell in a heap, laughing and crying.

Finally we came to our senses. "Sallie, it's you! I can't believe it. When did you get here? *How?*"

We talked and talked; we tried to tell her how — and why. She was glad to see us and she'd take time off from work and show us a real good time in

Chicago — *but*. The "but" was that we first had to call our parents.

I knew we'd have to do that; on the road, while we were in those cars, I'd rehearsed the call home. I'd tried to figure out a way not to call, but there wasn't any.

"You'll have to call first," said Sue.

And I knew I had to. After all, I had gotten Sue into this. She hadn't wanted to come and I had talked her into it. I'd have to tell my parents that, because they would want to blame Sue.

I picked up the phone and made the call collect. It rang only twice and then I heard my father's voice.

"Dad, it's me. Sallie."

"Sallie — my God, where are you?"

"In Chicago with Anne. Sue is with me."

"But why? Why didn't you tell us? How did you get there?"

I could hear myself swallow. "By bus. We're fine. And we hitchhiked some."

"My God, Sallie . . ." and then his voice choked up and my mother was on the phone.

117

"Sallie, you're all right?"

"I'm fine. We're here at Anne's. We'll call Sue's parents. I knew you'd worry."

"We'll come after you. Your father and I will start right now and drive to Chicago."

"But we only just got here."

"We'll be there. Do you have any money? And what about clothes? You are all right?" Her voice sounded terribly fast and anxious and tight.

"I'm fine," I said, and I felt tired, too tired to say any more.

My father's voice was back at my ear. "Now you stay right there, Sallie. We'll fly up tomorrow and bring you back." It was his voice, but it was different. I wasn't afraid of anything he could say.

"We'd like to stay a couple of days," I said.

"Sallie, how could you? Anne is working. She doesn't have time for you."

"Yes, she does. It's fine with her. But we do need some money. We'll come back at the end of the week."

"Your mother won't like it."

"She'll understand," I said, and I hoped very much that she would.

"Sallie, I'll send you a check and please, you won't hitchhike back?"

"We'll take the bus. I promise."

There were warnings about the big city and advice on what to do and wear. What I remember most is my father saying, "Please," and sounding as if he meant it.

Then it was Sue's turn.